For my children, Sam, Helen, and William
H.B.

For my daughter Luba with much love
M.S.

Consultant:
Daniel Simmonds
Gorilla Keeper, ZSL London Zoo

First American edition published in 2009
by Boxer Books Limited.

Distributed in the United States and Canada by
Sterling Publishing Co., Inc.
387 Park Avenue South, New York, NY 10016-8810

First published in Great Britain in 2009
by Boxer Books Limited.
www.boxerbooks.com

The illustrations were prepared using acrylic paints and soft pencil.
The text is set in Adobe Garamond.

ISBN 13: 978-1-906250-26-3

1 3 5 7 9 10 8 6 4 2

Printed in China

All of our papers are sourced from managed forests and renewable resources.

GORILLA'S STORY

WRITTEN BY HARRIET BLACKFORD

ILLUSTRATED BY MANJA STOJIC

BOXER BOOKS

Gorilla peeks out from his mother's big, strong arms. His bright eyes stare out from his small, black, hairy face.

All around him, Gorilla can hear the soft sounds of munching as the gorillas forage for food deep in the African forest.

As Gorilla grows bigger, he wants to explore. He holds on to his mother's long, black hair and crawls down to the ground. Gorilla's mother keeps her eye on him but scoops him up when the group moves on.

Gorilla's father is the biggest gorilla in the group. He has a big, black, hairy chest and a silvery white back.

It takes Gorilla a long time to learn to walk on his own. But now he is almost a year old and can also climb trees! His favorite thing to do is to ride on his mother's back, then leap off onto his friends and roll around wrestling.

Gorilla still drinks his mother's milk, but now that he is getting bigger, he likes to try everything the grown-ups eat. The forest provides all the leaves, shoots, stems, and fruit he needs to grow as big and strong as his father, the silverback.

Before the sun sets each day the gorillas build nests for sleeping. Gorilla has grown big enough to build his own nest.

He pulls down branches and leaves and bends them to fit underneath him. Gorilla's nest is not as neat as his mother's, but it is all his own work.

One day Gorilla and his group come to a big, open area of the forest. Here they meet other gorilla groups. But since there are enough juicy plants for everyone, they are all happy to eat together.

Gorilla has found a patch of really tasty stems. He is so busy chewing that he does not notice a pair of yellow eyes watching him from the forest.

Suddenly a huge leopard leaps toward Gorilla out of the trees. Gorilla screams and runs. His father hears him and rushes at the leopard, roaring and barking loudly. The frightened leopard slinks back into the forest and disappears.

Gorilla has become very big now. His father did not want another big strong male in his group, so Gorilla does not travel with them anymore. One day, all alone, Gorilla comes upon a very large group, led by an old silverback male.

Some young females move close to
Gorilla to eat. Gorilla struts around
to show how strong he's grown.

The big old silverback watches
Gorilla. Then suddenly he rushes
at Gorilla with a terrible roar.

Gorilla does not run away but stands
up and beats his chest. He is bigger
and stronger than this old gorilla.

The two gorillas look at one another for a while. Then the old gorilla sits down and starts munching on some leaves. Gorilla does the same but keeps his eye on the old male.

The sun is going down, and it's time to build a nest for the night. Gorilla gets up to go, and some of the young females follow him. He waits for them to catch up. The old silverback moves on with the rest of his group, ignoring Gorilla.

Gorilla has his own group to look after now.
He is strong enough to protect them and knows
where there are tasty plants to eat. It will not be
long before Gorilla has his own babies to look
out for in the thick, leafy forests of Africa.

Gorillas

A note from the author

Gorillas learn to take care of themselves as they grow up, just as children do. A young gorilla has to learn how to live among other gorillas, just as children have to learn how to live with other people in their community. This book tells the story of one gorilla and how he grew up.

Here are some facts about gorillas: Gorillas are the biggest apes alive today. Apes include gorillas, chimpanzees, orangutans, and man—that means you! Apes are the most intelligent of all animals, with a larger brain-for-body size than any other animal. Gorillas can learn hundreds of words in sign language and even put some together to make phrases.

Gorillas are strong, heavy animals. A big male can weigh more than two grown-up men. The females are much smaller, being half the size of the males. Gorillas eat the leaves, shoots, stems, and fruits of particular plants found in their forest home. Sometimes they also eat small animals such as insects. Gorillas need to eat for most of the day to get enough energy to live, and to do this they need very strong jaws and teeth. The male gorilla in particular has extremely big canine teeth. He needs big, strong muscles to work his jaws and a big skull to anchor these muscles. This is why his head is dome shaped.

Male gorillas grow a silvery white band of hair across their backs as they mature, which is why they are called "silverbacks." Gorillas live in groups led by a silverback, with some females and their young and sometimes other young males, if the leader is happy for them to stay with him. The silverback protects his group from dangers such as predators, hunters, and other male gorillas, who would want to take over his group. He does this by standing up and beating his chest while roaring and barking. He also rushes at the danger, tearing up the vegetation as he goes. At times like this he uses his huge canine teeth if he has to. This behavior makes the gorilla seem fierce, but every year thousands of tourists are taken to within a few feet of wild gorillas as they go about their lives.

Gorillas are found only in a small area of Africa. There are two species, the Western gorilla and the Eastern gorilla, which includes the Mountain gorilla. They are an endangered species, which means there are not many left in the wild. One problem for them is the cutting down of trees for wood and to make space for agriculture. This leaves the gorilla with nowhere to forage for food. Roads made by the loggers allow hunters easy access to the remote places where gorillas live, and many are killed for "bush meat." Tourism may help protect gorillas, because people want to see them in the wild. But this leads to another problem: gorillas may catch our germs and get sick. A lot needs to be done to save this amazing animal from extinction. Maybe one day you can help save the gorilla.